D0508092

Raintree is an imprint of Capstone Global Library Limited, a company
incorporated in England and Wales having its registered office at 7
Pilgrim Street, London, EC4V 6LB - Registered company number: 6695582

www.raintree.co.uk
myorders@raintree.co.uk

Designed by Hilary Wacholz
Original illustrations © Capstone 2016
Illustrated by Kirbi Fagan
Design Elements: Shutterstock: Epsicons, NEGOVURA, squarelogo,
punsayaporn, Catz, MaluStudio, In·Finity

ISBN 978 1 4747 1047 3 (paperback)
19 18 17 16 15
10 9 8 7 6 5 4 3 2 1

British Library Cataloguing in Publication Data
A full catalogue record for this book is available from
the British Library.

Printed and bound in China.

TORNADO

A TWISTING TALE OF SURVIVAL

> BY THOMAS KINGSLEY TROUPE

> ILLUSTRATED BY KIRBI FAGAN

SURVIVE!

raintree
a Capstone company — publishers for children

CONTENTS

> **CHAPTER 1**
THE TOWER.......................... 6

> **CHAPTER 2**
OLD ROAD 12

> **CHAPTER 3**
ANGRY SKIES 17

> **CHAPTER 4**
GO! GO! GO! 23

> **CHAPTER 5**
TOWN DOWN 28

> **CHAPTER 6**
MAD DASH 34

> **CHAPTER 7**
LAST DITCH 39

> **CHAPTER 8**
BLOWN AWAY 44

THE TOWER

Tony Shermer and his twin sister, Andie, stared intently at their cabin's picnic table. They studied the map their dad had spread out like they were planning a ground assault that would save the world from an alien attack.

Dad pointed at the map. "I'm pretty sure the tower is a few miles out this way," he said. "There was a lot of flooding back in the day. There's quite a few abandoned places out there."

Nice, Tony thought. *Exploring an abandoned ranger tower sounds pretty great.*

Andie chewed her gum and itched a mosquito bite on her shoulder. "Can we go and look for it?" she asked. "We could take the quad bikes out there."

Tony watched his dad glance up at the sky. Clouds blotted out the sun. "Looks like there's a storm coming."

"We'll head there and come straight back!" Andie pleaded. "A little rain never hurt anyone."

Dad smirked. "Yeah, that should be fine," he said. "Stick to the trails. You should be able to find it without too much trouble. Just be back in time for dinner. Joey wants us all to go and see the fireworks in town tonight."

Tony rolled his eyes. "Sure thing," he said. "We wouldn't want to miss that."

Tony had forgotten about the fireworks. Summer had that effect on him. The hot days up at the family cabin seemed to blend together. He and Andie started to find fireworks boring a few years ago. But his little five-year-old brother, Joey, still loved to see them.

"Oh, one last thing," Dad said, folding up the map. "The tower must be pretty old and tired by now. Don't try to climb it. Okay?"

"Did you hear that, Andie?" Tony said, smirking at his sister. "No daredevil stuff."

Andie popped her chewing gum. "Don't be such a chicken."

"Andrea," Dad said, his eyebrows furrowed.

"Okay, okay," Andie said. "I was joking." Then she winked at Tony.

Tony sighed.

★ ★ ★

Ten minutes later, Tony and Andie had started up their quad bikes, strapped their helmets on and taken off down the dirt trails. The wind rippled Tony's shirt and wafted the fishy smell of Lake Borden into his face. His legs shook as he bounded over little pits in the road.

Andie, as usual, was up ahead of him, racing just a little bit faster than Tony was willing to go.

Always pushing the pace, Tony thought. *My sister, the adrenaline junkie.*

To be fair, they were still on a familiar section of the trails that looped back towards the cabins. And Andie was no slouch on the quad bike, either. But it didn't take much to get thrown.

From what Tony saw on the map, there was supposed to be an old overgrown road just past the upcoming bend. He wasn't sure if Andie was looking for it, though. The way she was racing, she'd probably blast right past it.

Tony smirked inside his helmet. "Good," he said to himself.

Even though they never officially called their quad bike runs "races," Andie always won them. Every single time. As suspected, she reached the curve in the road and sped off, letting the fat tyres slide left as she rounded the bend.

Tony slowed down near a patch of grass that grew a bit differently. *It's the old road!* He realized.

Without slowing down, Andie looked back to see why Tony had stopped. He gave her a quick salute and turned off in the new direction. "Come and catch me, speedy," he whispered to himself.

Tony glanced up at the sky. The clouds were definitely darker, but he couldn't hear any thunder yet. Not over the sound of his engine anyway.

Tony looked down just in time to duck his head. A few low-hanging branches scratched his helmet. The road barely resembled a path anymore. If it weren't for the twin tyre grooves worn into the soil, it'd be easy to get lost.

Tony scanned the area for landmarks. *Now where's this abandoned tower...*

CHAPTER 2

OLD ROAD

Tony decelerated a little and glanced behind him. Andie was right on his tail, ducking and dodging the obstacles the old path threw at her. He knew she was aching to catch up with him, which made him just a little bit happy.

Nothing wrong with second place once in a while, sis, Tony thought. She always gave him a hard time for going slower, but he preferred to take his time and enjoy the rides. Not Andie, though. She even loved to remind him that she was born twelve minutes before he was.

They zipped through the overgrown trail until Tony had to stop abruptly. Andie revved her engine behind him in annoyance. He didn't want to imagine what she'd be like on the road once she'd got her driving license.

Tony cut the engine and climbed off his quad. "Stop," he yelled. "The road's blocked."

Andie hesitated, then cut her engine. "What is it?" she asked.

Tony knew it was torture for Andie to stay still for even a second. "Come and see for yourself," he said over his shoulder.

Andie groaned. "Fine," she said.

The twins stood in front of an old, rotten tree that lay across the twin ruts in the overgrown road. It looked like it had fallen decades ago. He kicked it with his tennis shoe, leaving a sizeable hole in the soggy bark.

Andie snapped her chewing gum. "Can we move it?" she asked.

"We can try," Tony said. "But it'll probably take a while."

Andie tilted her head at him. "You don't want to, do you?"

"What do you mean?" Tony asked.

Andie pointed. "You think it'll be too much hard work to move this thing."

"Well, it *is* a tree," Tony said.

"Yeah, but most of it is rotten," Andie said. "It can't be that heavy. Even if it is, we can just clear a path wide enough for us to pass through."

Tony frowned. "Maybe," he said. "There might be a storm coming, you know."

"You just want an excuse to go back," Andie said. "Don't you want to see that tower?" She grinned at her twin. "Seriously, Tony. Live a little."

Tony grinned back. She always knew just what to say to egg him on. "Fine," he said. "Let's get to work."

Andie nudged past Tony and crouched down. She yanked on a giant chunk of rotten tree. It came away more easily than she'd expected, sending squirmy bugs flying everywhere.

"Ah!" Andie yelped, brushing them off her trousers.

"Relax, sis," Tony said. "They're just bugs. Live a little."

Andie grunted. "Oh, be quiet."

Together, with minimal sibling rivalry, the two of them cleared away enough of the tree to continue their journey.

As they hopped back onto their quads, Tony thought he heard a distant rumble of thunder. He didn't dare say anything to Andie, though. She'd just tease him about being afraid of loud noises.

We'll just find the tower, take a quick look and head back, he told himself. *Hopefully before the storm...*

CHAPTER 3

ANGRY SKIES

They raced past a number of old, abandoned cabins on the old road. Some of them were completely overrun with plants. Some were missing windows and looked like they would be great sets for horror films. Tony wondered how long ago there had been families like his living there, enjoying a barbecue and swimming in the lake.

Twenty minutes later, he forgot all about the cabins. Ahead of them – like an ancient, wooden finger reaching towards the sky – was the abandoned ranger tower.

"Punch it, Anthony!" Andie yelled from behind him. "We're almost there!"

Tony wanted to ignore her, which he'd learned over time was usually the wisest course of action. But instead he zipped down another turn, bounded over a downed, weather-worn fence and made a bee-line to the base of the tower. He came to a stop just beneath the tower and turned off the engine.

Tony took off his helmet and climbed off his quad. "Nice," he whispered.

Andie pulled up alongside him.

"For the record," Tony said without taking his eyes off the tower, "I won."

"Oh, whatever," Andie said. "We weren't even racing, *little brother.*"

Tony ignored the teasing and let his eyes wander up the length of the tower. It'd been built with dark, stained wood, and stood at least thirty metres tall. Staircases zigzagged back and forth all the way up to the hatch in the tower's floor.

Tony noticed that more than a few of the wooden steps were missing, rotten or broken.

"Why did they even build this thing?" Andie asked. She walked underneath the tower, kicking through the tall grass. Tony hoped Andie was just taking a closer look, but he knew better.

Tony followed her. "They build them so park rangers can spot fires and stuff from a distance, I think," he said. He noticed for the first time how dark the sky had grown. The clouds were puffy and grey. As if on cue, a quick flash of lightning lit up the sky.

"We have to climb this thing," Andie said, ignoring the brewing storm. "Seriously."

"No way," Tony said. "I know you just saw the lightning. We've got to get back, and quickly!"

"A little rain has never hurt anyone," Andie said. "Plus, we've only just got here."

Not even twenty seconds later, the rain came pouring down.

The two of them were soaked in seconds. They ran beneath the wooden tower supports for shelter.

It didn't help much.

"This stinks," Tony said, raindrops slapping at his skull. "We're at least a forty-minute drive from our cabin. There's nowhere to go."

"Town can't be too far away," Andie said, shielding her eyes from the rain. "Anyway, I'm sure it will blow over any minute now."

Tony groaned. It was going to be miserable trying to get back to their cabin through the overgrown road with all the wet branches and mud. As interesting as the tower was, he really wished he was back inside their cabin where it was dry.

Almost as soon as it had started, the rain stopped. The sky had turned pale green. Random drops fell from the soaked wooden structure towering above them. The air around them was calm. Eerily calm.

"Told you it would blow over," Andie said. She cracked her knuckles. "Time to scale this monster."

"Are you insane?" Tony said. "The stairs are falling apart!"

"Just a little," Andie admitted. "But it's sturdy enough. I'll be fine."

Tony knew there was no stopping her. He stood in the wet grass and watched his sister make her way to the first set of steps.

That was when Tony heard a train approaching in the distance.

CHAPTER 4

GO! GO! GO!

Tony hadn't seen any train tracks this far north, and he'd never heard trains in his previous visits to the family cabin. *What's making that noise, then?* he thought.

Tony's eyes went wide and his heart skipped a beat. "Andie!" he shouted. "We've got to go! *NOW!*"

"Wow, settle down," Andie said. She was already two flights up. Tony saw the rotten wood bend a little beneath her foot. A moment later, she took a big step over a missing wooden plank. "I said I'd be fine, and I am. Relax."

Tony looked up at the sky. The clouds were moving with alarming quickness, and the train-like sound was getting louder. He strapped his helmet back on as the wind whipped against his face. He hopped onto his quad bike, anxious to go.

"Andie, seriously!" Tony shouted. "You need to get down! I think there's a –"

"TORNADO!" Andie cried. For the first time in his life, Tony saw fear on his sister's freckled face.

Andie began stomping down the steps. As she got to the last flight of stairs, a rotten plank snapped in half. She tumbled forward and landed hard on her back in the tall grass beneath the tower.

Tony ran over to her. He started to ask if she was okay, but Andie leapt back to her feet like falling had all been part of her plan.

"I'm fine," she muttered. There was a little blood trailing from a long scrape on her leg, but nothing his rugged sister hadn't experienced before. She scrambled over to her quad and casually threw her leg over to climb on.

"You've forgotten your helmet," Tony said.

The wind was howling like crazy. Tony looked up at the sky. Leaves rippled in the trees, filling the air with a chittering sound. He glanced at his sister. "Did you really see a tornado?" he asked.

"Oh, yeah," Andie said quickly. She pulled the helmet onto her wet hair. "A *big* one."

Without another word, they fired up their engines and accelerated down the overgrown trail.

"Where are we going to go?" Andie shouted.

Tony considered their options. He had no idea if the tornado was coming their way, but he also knew it would take a little under an hour to get back to their cabin. They were much closer to Branson, the nearby small town where they bought their groceries and petrol.

"How far away was the tornado?" Tony shouted.

"A fair way off – but it seemed to be heading towards us," Andie shouted back. "Shouldn't we just head in the other direction?"

Tony wasn't sure. He knew it would be dangerous to stay out in the open during a storm. Beyond that, he thought he remembered hearing that the best thing to do was lie down in a field or a ditch, and wait out the storm. But there was nothing like that anywhere near by.

"I'm not sure," Tony yelled. "Maybe we –"

CRACK! The sound of snapping timber came from behind them. With a quick glance over his shoulder, Tony saw the ranger tower begin to lean. Less than two seconds later, the entire structure had toppled over. It fell into the woods two metres or so behind them, stripping branches from trees and landing with a crash on the overgrown trail they'd just left.

"Forget that!" Andie cried out. "Let's head for Branson!"

Tony nodded, lowered his head and revved the quad's engine. He blasted along the trail, kicking up mud and grass behind him.

CHAPTER 5

TOWN DOWN

The wind was picking up. Tony wondered if they'd get pulled off the ground and up into the sky. He couldn't see the twister through all the trees, but Tony decided that must be a good thing. If they saw it, then it'd already be too late.

We'll make it to town before then, he thought.

He and Andie emerged from the overgrown road back onto the main trail. Tony took a sharp left and ripped his way up the hill. His wheels struggled through the mud a little. Andie's quad caught up, and she rode next to him.

"I think it's gone, Tony," Andie said, looking off towards where the tower had been. "I can't see it anymore."

"I don't know," Tony said. His heart was still pounding in his chest like a piston. Something in the air just didn't feel right. They still had a little way to go before they'd reach Branson. To be safe, they needed to get to a basement.

"Tony?" Andie said, waving her hand in his face. "Earth to Tony, snap out of it!"

Tony shook his head to clear it. He nodded towards the road. "Either way, we should keep heading towards Branson," he said.

They raced down the trail, eventually passing the long-abandoned site of Camp Ludwig. With all the empty swimming pools and abandoned cabins, the property looked like a tiny ghost town. Some buildings looked ready to collapse.

"Almost at Branson," Tony shouted. His sister nodded.

As they finally reached the top of the ascent, Tony hit the brakes. A second later, Andie skidded to a stop next to him.

"No way," Andie whispered.

Both of them stared wide-eyed at the town. The tornado had beaten them to Branson.

* * *

Tony slumped into the seat of his idling quad. The tornado had been enormous – at least half a block wide based on the path of destruction.

At the far edge of town, Tony watched the tornado spin and snake its way along a wavy path through the outer edge of Branson. Trees were uprooted and flung like a toddler playing with vegetables. Shingles flew off of the roofs of houses. The cladding from houses was stripped away and flung skywards.

A large pick-up rolled end over end, a red blur of crunching glass and crumpling metal, until it smashed into the side of the town hall.

A moment later, the sheeting from the building's roof came off like the lid off a can. Bicycles, garden furniture, a bird bath and rubbish bins – too many things to count were flying about in the air.

Most of the town's houses were decimated, along with the neighbouring shops. Tony shuddered, wondering if the people had managed to get to safety in time.

A van with its alarm blaring caught Tony's attention. It flew through the sky like an invisible hand was lifting it up. Half a second later, the car disappeared into a fenced-in garden.

Andie pointed down the road. "Oh, no!" she cried.

Tony followed her finger. A golden retriever was running back and forth across the street, clearly terrified. All sorts of rubbish rained down around the dog. It zigged and zagged, heading one direction, then another.

"He's got the right idea," Tony said. "We have to get out of here."

Andie nodded, her eyes lingering on the dog. When Tony saw she wasn't moving, he nudged her in the ribs.

"There's nothing we can do for him," Tony said. "But we have to –"

"I know, I know, we've got to get out of here," Andie said sadly. Her voice rose when she added, "I bet one of those old cabins by the lake has a basement! It's worth a shot!"

Tony nodded. "Good call," he said.

Tony turned the handlebars of his quad bike and hit the accelerator ... and felt the engine splutter and then die.

"Let's go, bro," Andie said. "Move it!"

Tony tried to restart the engine. And again. The wind picked up behind him. As he tried to start the engine once again, he heard trees at the edge of town snap like twigs underfoot.

"I can't get the engine to start!" Tony yelled.

CHAPTER 6

MAD DASH

"Get on!" Andie shouted.

Tony tried to start his engine one last time so they could ride away together. Nothing happened. *Dead,* he thought.

Tony grunted and jumped off his quad bike. A moment later, he was seated behind his sister on her quad, his hands gripping the back rack tightly. She turned sharply and revved the engine, spinning them back onto the trail. Back the way they'd come.

"I'm in first place again," Andie shouted as they took off.

Tony smirked – and held on for dear life. Andie drove like a maniac under normal circumstances. With a deadly tornado thrown into the mix, Tony realized she'd been holding back.

In minutes, Tony's neck was sore from the wind slapping against his helmet. Branches and loose debris from Branson pelted him from every side. The roar of the funnel cloud was nearly deafening. For the first time since the storm began, Tony wondered if they were going to survive.

A tree fell into the road just ahead of them. "Hang on!" Andie cried. She veered sharply, guiding them into a ditch. The off-road was bumpy, forcing Tony to grip the back rack even more tightly.

Tony heard a big, metal crunch behind him. As he turned back to look, the landscape changed before his eyes. Trees toppled smaller ones, which were then tossed into the air. With utter disbelief, Tony watched his abandoned quad bike disappear into the funnel cloud.

I hope Dad insured that thing, Tony thought.

"Will we make it to the cabins?" Andie cried, her voice stuttering from bumps in the ditch. "It sounds like this twister is getting closer every second!"

Tony didn't know what to say. At any moment, a tree could tip over and smash them into the ground. Getting to the cabins in time was the last thing on his mind.

"We just need to find a basement or something underground!" Tony said.

"I hope you brought a shovel," Andie said. "We're a bit short on basements out here!"

Tony grinned. He was about to respond when he noticed a worn sign up ahead. In faded, stencilled letters were the words CAMP LUDWIG.

"Turn here!" Tony said. "Maybe we can find shelter at the camp." It was a long shot, but it was their only option. The abandoned cabins were too far away, and the twister was right on their heels.

Andie turned without argument. Tony held on tight as the quad's fat tyres bounded over the rough ground towards the campsite.

The dingy little buildings up ahead looked sad and small, seemingly cowering in fear.

"Stop!" Tony cried. The quad bike tore up a huge swatch of grass as they jerked to a halt. They hopped off the quad and ran to a nearby cabin.

Andie looked the little structure up and down. "Is there a basement?" she asked.

The wind howled around them. Trees fell near by. Tony spotted a small window near the bottom of the side of the cabin. He ran over, dropped down onto his bottom, and kicked with both feet. The old wood broke apart, shattering the glass.

"Yes!" Tony said. "Let's go!"

He poked his head in through the dusty, cobwebbed hatch and looked around. *Oh, no,* he thought.

Tony pulled his head out. "There's no basement!" he shouted to his sister. "It's just a crawlspace!"

CHAPTER 7

LAST DITCH

All Tony had seen inside were a bunch of wooden beams, some rusty pipes and what he could only imagine were animal nests. There wasn't any more protection inside than there would be in the rickety old cabin itself.

As Tony brushed the cobwebs from his hair, he saw Andie scanning the campsite, her eyes darting from building to building. She'd stopped chewing her gum, and her face was pale.

Tony glanced around at the other cabins as well. To his dismay, he saw that all of them were built the same way. Every single one had a crawl space. *No basements,* he realized.

The wind grew even stronger. Tony knew their time was almost up.

"You saw what that thing did to the town," Tony said. "These flimsy cabins won't keep us safe."

Andie nodded. "So let's get back on and drive away from here," she said. "That thing is going to be here any second!"

They turned to run towards the quad just in time to see a cabin at the outer edge of the campsite explode in a cloud of splinters and shingles. Pieces of wood whistled through the air, one of which embedded itself in the neighbouring cabin.

Tony tugged his sister by the arm and said, "Run!" Andie ran alongside him, and the two headed towards the other side of the campsite. Another cabin fell beneath the tornado. Chunks of debris and leaves swirling around them made it nearly impossible to see where they were going.

Tony squinted. A large, rectangular opening in the ground lay up ahead.

"The pool!" Tony shouted. He ran faster while making sure Andie stayed in front of him. "Get in!"

"Are you serious?" Andie shouted back. "How will that help us?"

"It's below ground!" Tony said. He grabbed his sister by the arm and they reached the edge of the pool. There, along the side, was a faded number 9. Together, they dropped over the edge. The bottom of the pool was filled with old, soggy leaves, a few plastic cups and a pathetic, deflated beach ball.

"Get your back against the side," Tony shouted.

"We're sitting ducks here!" Andie cried.

Tony grinned, remembering the mock drills they'd had in the basement of their school. "Then play the part: Sit down and duck your head!"

Andie gave him an incredulous look. "You're crazy!" she said, but she did what he'd suggested.

The two of them curled up and pulled their heads down between their knees, covering their helmets with their arms.

Above them, Tony heard what remained of the campsite being torn to shreds. Cabin walls flew over their heads, raining chunks of wood on them. A canoe smashed into the lip of the pool and split in half, the remains landing within a metre of them.

The wind was unbelievable. Tony felt his body shifting back and forth despite his best efforts to stay still. He held his breath, certain he and Andie would be pulled up into the sky and tossed somewhere into the woods.

As the tornado swirled near them, he felt the incredible wind pressure squishing him against the side of the pool. Tony struggled to turn his head. He saw the base of the tornado rip through the nearest cabins and trees, erasing them with destructive force.

And it was heading straight for the pool.

Tony closed his eyes. "Hold on!" he cried, his voice barely audible through the blasting winds. "It's coming for us!"

Andie didn't respond.

CHAPTER 8

BLOWN AWAY

After what seemed like forever, the air started to settle. Everything around Tony fell silent. He kept his head down, too afraid to look up and see that his sister was gone.

Then he heard Andie laughing. "Oh, wow," she said. "What a rush!"

Tony lifted his head and opened his eyes. His crazy sister was lying on her back next to him. She didn't seem to care about the wet, leafy sludge that lined the bottom of the pool. There were at least three cabins' worth of destroyed lumber scattered around the remains of the camp's canoe.

Tony let out a sigh of relief. "Now who's the crazy one?" he asked.

Andie continued to chuckle while looking up at the sky; it seemed to Tony like she was laughing in its face. She dabbed the cut on her leg. Amazingly, neither of the twins had been otherwise injured.

"We made it," Tony said, smiling.

"That thing was after us," Andie said. "It was like it didn't want us messing with the ranger tower, and it was cross."

"Tornadoes are unpredictable," Tony said with a shrug.

"Whatever, brainiac," Andie said. "That twister was out for our blood."

Tony shook his head. He'd let her think what she wanted. What mattered was that they were alive. His mind wandered to the people in Branson, which made him suddenly think of...

"Our cabin," Tony said. "*Dad*."

Andie went pale. "I hope he's all right," she said quietly.

Within minutes, the twins climbed out of the pool and made their way through the rubble, heading for the main path.

★ ★ ★

Walking through the woods wasn't easy. But after an hour and a half of lifting, jumping and climbing, Tony and Andie Shermer finally found their dad's cabin.

And it was still in one piece.

Their little brother raced across the damp garden towards them. "Hey you two" Joey shouted. "You missed it! We saw a tornado!"

Dad emerged from the doorway, relief washing over his face. He joined Joey and the twins in the front garden.

"Yeah," Tony said, ruffling Joey's hair. "We saw it too."

Once Dad had finished obsessively checking the twins for injuries, they told him about their adventure.

"I was worried sick," Dad said. "I heard from the neighbours what happened to Branson. We were worried that you'd ended up there."

"Almost," Andie said. "We saw the tornado chew that place up and spit it out."

Tony hung his head. "We lost both of the quads, Dad," he said.

Their dad shrugged. "Don't care," he said warmly. "As long as you two are safe. Quad bikes are replaceable. My twins aren't."

Andie chuckled. "We should get faster ones, actually," she said. "That tornado almost caught up with us."

Tony had to admit it: his sister was fearless.

Dad smiled and playfully socked Andie in the shoulder. "I thought I told you no daredevil stuff," he said.

"In her defence, Dad," Tony said, "she didn't have much of a choice this time."

Andie smiled from ear to ear.

★ ★ ★

That night, the four of them lit fireworks on their dock. Joey ran along the beach with a sparkler. Understandably, Branson cancelled the fireworks – but the Shermers made do with what they had.

"After today, fireworks seem even more boring," Andie said. She held a sparkler in her hand. Little flecks of light popped and fizzed from the metal stick. A bandage was wrapped around her leg.

"Yeah," Tony said. "But I'm quite happy with boring for a while."

What his sister said next was more shocking to Tony than anything that had happened in the last twenty-four hours.

"Yeah," Andie said. "Me too."

SURVIVING A TORNADO

Despite what you may have heard, tornadoes can happen at any time. They're usually invisible until they pick up dust, objects and other debris, so if you can see a tornado, then you're already in danger. Therefore it is important to be prepared for whenever early warning signs appear.

PREPARATION

- With your family, choose an emergency safe space that's away from windows. A cellar, or bathroom at or below ground level is best.
- Decide in advance who will bring your pets to the safe space.
- Identify where utility shut-offs are located, including gas, electricity and water. Ensure you have the necessary tools near by to shut them off before the tornado hits. Decide who will shut them off.

- Keep a fully stocked first aid kit, torches and batteries near by.
- Above all else, determine if your city or town has a designated safe place or shelter – and how far away from home it's located.

Warning signs

A dark, pale green sky can be an indicator of a tornado. Other signs include heavy hail, dark and low-lying clouds and a roaring sound in the air. When any of these appear, begin your preparations! Lastly, make sure you keep an eye on weather watches via television, radio or SMS alerts (text messages). A Tornado Warning means that a tornado is on the ground or has been detected. Seek shelter immediately!

During the tornado

If you get caught in a tornado outside your home, don't stay inside a car or try to outrun the tornado. If you're outside, find an open field or low-lying ditch that is far away from items that could injure you if flung around by the tornado. Crouch down, lie flat and wait out the storm.

After the storm

Don't return to your house or go outside until the all-clear has been given! Make sure to document all damage to your house and belongings with a digital camera. That way, filing an insurance claim will be easier.

ABOUT THE AUTHOR

Thomas Kingsley Troupe has written more than thirty children's books. His book *Legend of the Werewolf* (Picture Window Books, 2011) received a bronze medal for the Moonbeam Children's Book Award. Thomas lives in Minnesota, USA, with his wife and two sons.

ABOUT THE ILLUSTRATOR

Kirbi Fagan is a vintage-inspired artist living in the Detroit, Michigan area of the USA. She is an award-winning illustrator who specializes in creating art for young readers. Her work is known for magical themes, vintage textures, bright colours and powerful characterization. She received her bachelor's degree in Illustration from Kendall College of Art and Design. Kirbi lives by two words: "Spread joy". She is known to say, "I'm in it with my whole heart". When not illustrating, Kirbi enjoys writing stories, spending time with her family and rollerblading with her dog, Sophie.

GLOSSARY

abandoned left alone, or left behind without care or protection

adrenaline substance that is released in the body of a person who is feeling excitement, fear or anger. It causes the heart to beat more quickly and gives the person more energy.

casually without much effort or concern

minimal very small or slight in size or amount

overgrown covered with plants that have grown in an uncontrolled way

rivalry state of competition

soggy soaked with water

timber wood from a tree, or a tree that may one day be used as wood for building something

WRITING PROMPTS

1. After reading the tornado survival tips at the end of the story, what do you think the siblings in this story should have done differently? Make a list of things they could have done – or not done – to increase their chances of survival.

2. Write a short story about surviving a different kind of natural disaster. What happens? How do you survive it? Write about it.

3. Create your own preparation plan for a tornado. List all the members of your family, including pets. Assign responsibilities to each person and explain why. Where would the safest place in your house be? If you live in a flat, is there a tornado shelter?

DISCUSSION QUESTIONS

1. Which sibling in this story do you like the most? Why? Discuss your reasons.

2. Do you or your family go to cabins or go camping on holiday? If you could go anywhere, where would you choose to go on holiday?

3. Which illustration in this book is your favourite? Why?